# Pipe Dream

## C.M.Williams

2026 Edition – Published by Rindmark – http://www.rindmark.art

Cover design and artwork by C.M.Williams

Diz Williams Tattoo – http://www.dizwilliamstattoo.com

# Contents

# CHAPTER ONE

# Forty–Seven Hours

He hadn't slept in forty-seven hours when he first saw her.

No falling sensation, no cut from one place to another. One second Jake was watching the hairline crack above his kitchen light, the next he was sitting in a long, coin-operated laundromat that hummed like a beehive.

The vending machine rattled.

Rows of silver drums turned slow as planets.

He lifted his mug—still warm from hours of wakefulness—and found his tea: chamomile, the same boring concoction he used as a potion to steal even one lousy wink. Steam without taste, like the memory of what rest used to feel like.

"This dream has a terrible budget," he said to no one, looking around.

"Hey!" a voice answered from behind a dryer. "Don't insult my imagination!" A giggle followed.

She shuffled into view wearing pink cloud-print pyjama bottoms and a jumper three washes past decent, barefoot, hair knotted in a messy bun with purpose. A paintbrush speared through the bun like a flagpole. She carried a chipped mug that said NAP QUEEN in gold that used to shimmer.

"You're not supposed to be here." She narrowed her eyes, amused.

"I could say the same." He smirked, palms open in surrender. "Usually it's me and the ceiling."

"Pfft. The ceiling's overrated." She rolled her eyes, remembering every morning she'd woken to its dull stare. She slid onto the plastic chair opposite him and tucked one leg beneath the other, wincing. A constellation of fresh and fading bruises dotted her shin like a Jackson Pollock. She caught him noticing and tugged her pant cuff down.

"Heh, I fall a lot," she said with a shrug. "Keeps me on my toes."

Jake let out a small puff of air and nodded. "So, what's your story then?" He smiled, then sobered. "Mine's insomnia. I have to drink this crap just to see the backs of my eyelids... and now you, apparently."

She raised her eyebrows, interested. "Oh wow, that explains the crap. Well, my cup of crap is coffee. I can't even taste it anymore, let alone enjoy the aroma." She traced her finger around the mug's rim and giggled. "Anyway... mine's narcolepsy."

"Oh, we're opposites?" he asked.

"We're a punchline," she corrected.

He leaned forward to rest his mug on the floor, then crossed his arms boldly, ankle balanced on his knee—curious in spite of himself. "Alright. Which is worse?"

A slow spark lit her face. "Oooo, aren't you smug?" she teased, bobbing her head like a metronome.

He stayed leaning back, a grin tugging one corner of his mouth, patient for her move.

"What, we're doing this? Fine. You first." She gestured for him to begin.

"Okay, so..." He clapped his hands together, rubbing them like a fly sizing up a pastry. "Insomnia," he announced, squinting theatrically. "You never rest. Your thoughts grow teeth that bite you in the ass. Time stops making sense. You're too tired to sleep and too awake to live." He opened both palms—case closed. "Eh?" He leaned back, smug and waiting.

She tilted her head, unimpressed. "Narcolepsy. You drop mid-sentence, mid-staircase, mid-kiss. Woke up hugging a mailbox once. He wasn't my type. Mid-making coffee, mid-drinking coffee, and you wake up with burns." She spoke without looking away, confident she'd won.

He laughed, quick and surprised. "Ha! Well... the mailbox gets comedy points."

"Yeah? Well, insomnia gets poetry points—not bad for a guy in cufflinks." She smirked. "But poetry doesn't keep you from sleep-walking into traffic."

He considered her for a beat, the dryers' buzz filling the space between them. With his head bowed, one eye lifted, he pursed his lips. "Truce?"

She thought about it, then gave in. "Truce." She held out her hand.

His fingertips met hers but floated right through. They both blinked, puzzled, until a shared realisation washed over them—they were in dream-mode.

"Well, I'm Jake," he said, smiling.

"Posie." The name landed softly between them. She made a face. "Most people hear it and say, 'Like the flower?'"

"Like you," he said before he could stop himself.

She blinked, then let it go with a tiny sneer. "And you? Jake... hmm. How about Wakey Jakey?"

He chuckled. "Yeah? What about Dozy Posie?"

"Haha, sounds like a badly written children's book."

"I'd read it," he said kindly—too lightly—and tried not to look away when her eyes didn't.

The fluorescent light above them flickered. The drums slowed. Everything went a shade softer.

She yawned, the kind that folds a person in half, and when she straightened, she was already blurring at the edges.

"Well, I guess that's me. I don't always last long," she said, apologetic.

"Can't you stay?" he asked without thinking.

"I will if I can."

And with that, she vanished like warm breath on a cold window.

The hum went on.

# CHAPTER TWO

# Steam Without Taste

Jake woke, drowning in daylight and the hum of the fridge.

He lay there until the edges of the laundromat flaked off like paint in his mind—until even the trace of steam from an imaginary mug was gone.

The park outside his window was its usual patchwork of grass and shade; the crooked lamppost leaned the way it always had.

Jake rose, showered, shaved, and ironed a shirt he didn't need—just to feel sane. His hands remembered the ritual even while his head ran under a different sky. He poured herbal tea into a mug with a chip on the rim and watched the string fade into the water. The label promised calm.

"Well, this time you worked," he said. He didn't trust it, but he was glad it had done its job.

At work, Dave leaned over his partition with a tuna sandwich and eyebrows, spitting confetti over the cubicle.

"You look like a ghost, man," he exclaimed.

"Thanks. Wish I was one," Jake retorted.

"Big deadline?" Dave puffed through fish-covered teeth.

"Something like that."

He stared at the spreadsheet until the cells blurred into a portrait—messy bun, a paintbrush, and a bruise that looked like the thumbprint of a full moon.

By lunch he'd checked the conference-room window four times, scanning the patch of green below as if a girl in pyjamas might walk across it at noon and nod at him, like that was how the world worked.

He left the office early on the excuse of a headache. His boss took one look at him and kicked him out.

"Yes, go home, please! You're scaring the secretary, you ghoul," he joked, dismissing Jake with a light pat on the shoulder.

Jake stood at his kitchen counter with a blister pack of sleeping pills he'd bought in a brief fit of hope months ago.

He turned one over. It looked like a lie he wanted to believe. He swallowed it anyway.

At three in the morning, the pill was a joke he didn't laugh at. He sat by the glass with a cooling mug of tea, elbows denting the sill, the park wearing its cheap sodium halo. The swings creaked when the wind went through them, and that was almost her laugh. The crooked lamppost tilted its warm glow to one side of the park, swarmed by moths and midges hungry for light.

"Where are you, Dozy?" he sighed to his faint reflection, and the pane said nothing back except the foggy exhale disappearing like she did.

# CHAPTER THREE

## The Park Between

When sleep finally came the next night, it came like tide, not falling but erased by something larger—something peaceful, something wanted.

He opened his eyes inside the park. It was the picture of a late afternoon that wasn't. The crooked lamppost stood beside the bench, its wood scarred with carved initials — J + P. He didn't recall doing it, but his imagination must have. The swings creaked in a soft wind, everything in every detail in "wake." He knew this place from a thousand insomniac vigils, but it had never had a temperature before.

"Hey, stranger," Posie said, perched on the bench, bare feet scuffing the grass, pulling out blades with her toes.

"Hey, Dozy!" he said with a grin. Then, after a pause: "You're late."

"I napped through my alarm." She hopped down, winced, and tugged her sleeve to hide a new bruise on her wrist. "You look worse," she teased.

He laughed. "Yeah? Well, that's what being awake for a day and a half does to you."

Posie's eyes widened. "A day and a half? Oh man, if I had that, I might actually finish a painting in one sitting."

"Yeah, I get too much work done," he sighed.

"Oh, the perils of the big businessman," she teased, nudging his shoulder—her ghostly form passing right through him.

They sat. The greenery bustled with life. He could feel the warmth where their shoulders almost touched but never could.

"That lamppost," she said, looking up at the leaning light. "Looks like the one outside my place."

"It is outside my place," he said, and felt the world calmly fold itself in half. "I've been staring at this spot for years. I find comfort in it."

She went still in a way that wasn't sleep. "Heh, same. I haven't... gone out much," she said softly. "I'm scared of the stairs, of the curb, of the way the street hisses. Of myself."

He stared at the lamppost because he didn't know where else to put his eyes. "Well, seems like we're neighbours. We can just meet here." His kind, sunken eyes reassured her.

She shook her head. "I don't know how long I have. I was fluffing pillo—"

As if called by that, she flickered and vanished.

"I'll wait," he said into the air. She'll be back.

Seconds later, she snapped back like a skipped frame. "Oh! Well, that's new. A short one," she said, breathless and smiling. "Consider it suspense." She winked.

He exhaled what might have been a laugh. "You're going to be impossible to schedule."

"I like to keep my calendar open," she said, letting her head tip onto his shoulder as if she trusted him to be there when gravity wasn't. He didn't move, afraid of proving a worse outcome true.

# CHAPTER FOUR

# The Shape of Waiting

D ays grew paler. His flat became a waiting room — a lobby of boredom.

Chamomile mugs ringed his desk in faint yellow coins no sponge could fully remove.

He stopped going to work; just sat in his room on his bed, waiting — lingering in half-sleep for Posie.

Across the road, in an apartment he could never quite pick out by window, Posie began to write pieces of him down.

Bench. Lamppost. Chamomile. A laugh like rain. Hands tidy. Eyes kind but wrecked.

She taped the little list above her kettle for the hours when she was awake enough to be lonely and too awake to rest.

She started another painting — the park. Not a park, their park.

The sky bled where her wounds couldn't, and her hand refused to stop.

Sometimes, mid-brushstroke, she'd nod and slip.

Her arm would drag the brush straight down, leaving a torn Prussian-blue streak.

When she woke, she stared at that wild mark like a message.

She named those slashes for what she'd missed — his joke, the part about the mailbox, the way he looked at the lamppost not knowing what to say.

"Okay, well, that's the wind now," she told the painting.

She paused. "Hmm... maybe that's what it looks like here," she murmured, smiling to herself.

Months — weeks — dreams later, the park on the canvas began to look almost like the place in her head.

Sometimes she packed it in a tote bag with a bunny on it and carried it from bed to sofa to window, like a charm.

Every now and then, when she dozed off and he wasn't there, she'd wake and look at it.

She'd work on it a little bit more — more mistakes, more strokes, more breath and wind.

Her final draft was a little silhouette, a small shadow sitting on the bench; she painted him in like a photo — forever waiting for her — so when she was alone in that park, she could say she wasn't.

She wanted to gift it to him, but how?

She considered meeting him awake, but a wave of anxiety and concrete formed in her belly.

"No, no, no," she shuddered.

Entertaining the thought was one thing, but acting on it was dangerous — even for a bruised and battered hermit.

# Chapter Five

## *Tomorrow, Noon*

A year had passed like sand slipping through an hourglass. Hours turned into days, and weeks into months. One evening in the dream-park that was always four p.m., Jake arrived with his tie loosened and a thermos under his arm like a clumsy valentine.

"Promotion?" she asked, eyeing the tie.

He rubbed the back of his neck. "Yeah. I work from home now — can't stand that Dave guy. More money, same insomnia. I'm single-handedly keeping the herbal-tea industry alive."

"Good. Anything to help you sleep, so you can see me!" she said, swinging her legs like a little kid. "I've finished a painting!"

"Oh wow, good for you! May I see it?" he asked, looking around for any sign of it.

"Well, I would — I made it as a present, but I don't know how to get it to you."

Just as she spoke the last word, she flickered and vanished like smoke.

"Ha... okay, see you—" Mid-sentence she reappeared, as if time didn't make sense.

"Hi again!" she giggled, this time with a tote over her shoulder.

"Cute bunny. Reminds me of you," he said, hands buried in his pockets.

She pulled out the canvas but noticed it was smeared and blurred, like a distorted censor-bar.

"That's... nice?" he said, hesitating not to insult her work.

"Ha! No, this isn't what it really looks like. I guess we can't bring anything from the awake world into this one," she said, defeated.

"Hey, I still like your rainbow smudge," he said, and meant it.

They both chuckled, looking down.

He wanted to tell her he'd started watching the park more carefully — how he'd seen a woman in an upstairs window open her curtains when he did and stand there, holding a mug in both hands, like someone praying. But he didn't want to sound creepy — not in a place that didn't follow ordinary rules.

Instead he said, "Posie?"

"Mhm?"

"I'm tired of only meeting you here. I'd really like to see that painting."

She didn't pretend not to understand. Her shoulders rose and fell. "Jake... you know—"

"I want to see you when I can't sleep," he said, cutting her off. "I want to see you when I'm awake — to hold your..." He glanced down at her hands, then back up. "...your painting," he finished softly, like a shy little boy.

Her mouth did a small, brave thing. "I'm scared," she said. "You don't understand — I'm scared of how the concrete suddenly jumps at me. Of not making it past the door. Of falling in the road and waking up with gravel in my teeth. Of the noise everything makes." She lowered her head, legs trembling from remembered fear.

"It's just to the park — here, across the street," he said gently, because she was telling the truth. "It'll be okay. The bench. Noon. I'll be there. We can try. I—" He swallowed the rest. "I believe in you," he said, meeting her eyes.

She stared at the lamppost for a long moment, then at his face as if reading a sign in bad light. "Okay," she whispered, as if the word might break, and smiled. "Tomorrow. Noon."

"Tomorrow," he said, the leap in his voice making the park hold its breath as if it were listening.

He reached for her hand. Her fingers slid through his. They both sighed.

He almost took out what he'd brought in his pocket every night and never had the courage to finish — the small second-hand ring, silver, battered soft at the edges, the kind that says stay. But he didn't. He wanted her to see it when the light was awake.

"There's a question for you at noon — I need to say it face to face," he said softly, twiddling his fingers through her transparent hand. "But I need to hold this for real."

Posie looked puzzled. "Is this not face to face?" she giggled, unaware of the weight of the question.

"Not enough," he said softly, grazing her cheek with the back of his fingers — only close enough to feel the illusion without breaking it.

He stayed until even her echo felt like breathing.

Then the dream faded.

He caught, on her mouth, a smile that made room.

# CHAPTER SIX

# The Green Light

Morning came like a wave crashing, muted by walls.

Jake ironed a shirt he didn't need to wear and put on the coat he saved for days when he wanted to feel like a better man. He slipped the ring box into his pocket and palmed it twice, like checking a coin. The thermos he filled with chamomile—because he was a creature of ritual—and poured a capful, letting the steam write briefly in the air before giving it a gentle blow.

He arrived at the park at eleven, because noon was an hour for the brave, and he was not.

He sat on the bench, interlocking and unlocking his fingers, one leg jittering in rhythm with his nerves. The crooked lamppost leaned toward him as if it wanted to listen. He scanned the crossing for a sign of her, eyes drifting to the windows across the street—curtains drawn, indifferent.

He rehearsed lines and discarded them like napkins.

Hi. Too small.

Fancy meeting you here. Too lame.

Do we hug? Absolutely not.

The possibilities spun and tore through his thoughts like wind scattering paper.

He checked his watch.

11:57.

His heart beat so hard it felt tribal.

Posie silenced her alarm after the third buzz and lay still, listening to the house creak like something old and kind. She sat up, steadying herself with a hand on the wall.

"It's just to the park," she said aloud. "Just to the park. You can do this."

She exhaled through tight lips, a trembling, self-soothing breath.

She swapped slippers for sneakers, double-knotting the laces. Jeans. The jumper with paint freckles like stars. She lifted the tote holding her little painting and wondered what he'd think of it. If anything scared her more than leaving the house, it was the idea of him not liking it. But deep down, she knew he would.

She slipped her cracked phone into her pocket.

At the mirror, she dabbed concealer over a blossom of red beneath her cheekbone and laughed softly.

"He won't care," she told the glass. "He'll pretend he doesn't see."

Her phone buzzed.

12PM alarm — Meet up with Wakey Jakey.

She smiled. She put the phone away, gripped the handle, and opened the door. The stairwell smelled like dust and everyone's dinner from the night before.

She went down one flight, one hand on the rail. "Left foot, right foot," she murmured. "We like them both. We can do this."

At the landing, she paused and breathed through the tightening in her chest, the way her therapist had taught her.

Outside, the doorman blinked in surprise.

"Oh, Posie, isn't it?" he said.

"Hey, Jerry," she replied, grateful for the distraction.

"Haven't seen you down here in, what, eighteen months? Thought you'd moved out!" He chuckled at his own joke.

"Yeah, well, I missed the sun," she said, the lie tasting like dust.

They said their goodbyes, and she stepped into the light. The park was there—close enough to call to.

"Be kind," she whispered to the day. "It's just around the corner."

Jake poured a capful of tea he didn't drink. He imagined handing it to her.

Try it.

What is it?

A terrible habit.

He smiled at the thought, and then at nothing.

Noon came and went the way time does when you're lying in a field, watching clouds—too slowly, then all at once.

12:07. She was tying her laces, he told himself.

12:12. Maybe choosing a jumper.

12:15. He opened the ring box, closed it, opened it again—the hinge like a nervous heartbeat.

12:21. He stood to see better, though the corner café blocked his view.

12:30. Something in his chest tied itself into a knot and pulled tight.

He sat. Stood. Sat again. Watching the crossing like he could bend time by sheer will. His hands dug into his pockets until they hurt.

Posie reached the curb. The light blinked green.

"Almost there," she whispered.

The world began to tilt. Her legs grew heavy, her hands too light. The sound of the city—the hiss, the hum, the barking dog, the bicycle bell—rose and blurred, like water rushing past her ears.

"Not now," she begged. "Please... not now."

She stepped into the road, the tote thumping against her hip. The lamppost and Jake at the bench filled her mind. She was so focused on staying upright she didn't hear the car.

She turned, half-smiling, half-panicked—

"Oh—"

The word never finished.

Everything went black.

She slept for the last time.

At 12:50, Jake heard the sirens.

That far-away kind of close—the kind that's forty metres and forty kilometres all at once. He didn't move at first. Denial is a soft sound. Then came panic.

He listened harder, like listening might change the outcome.

By the time he ran, a small crowd had already gathered. Phones out. Hands over mouths. Some crying, some just... watching.

He pushed through, heart in his throat, praying it wasn't her. It was.

Posie lay bent and still, beautiful even in ruin. A canvas face-down beside her, the bunny tote turned inside out, flapping in the wind.

A splash of red—paint, or blood, he couldn't tell. The world became the sound people make when they're trying not to cry in public.

Someone was pressing on her chest. Someone else shouted into a phone. The sirens closed in.

Jake didn't speak. He didn't touch. He just stood there, surrounded by noise, feeling impossibly alone.

The taste of chamomile lingered in his mouth, and the question he didn't get to ask burned behind his teeth.

The ring in his pocket felt heavier than anything a pocket should ever carry.

# CHAPTER SEVEN

## The Colour Returns

That night, decided not to sleep.

Sleep came because the body shuts its doors when hallways fill with smoke.

He held the painting against his chest — the one streaked with blood, still faintly smelling of her — and a tear slipped down his cheek. Then he drifted off.

He opened his eyes in the park, though it wasn't how he remembered it.

It was always four o'clock there, but now the colour was gone.

The grass wore a dull grey, as if painted with the wrong brush.

The sky had no temperature, cold and empty.

The lamppost leaned, but not on purpose.

"Posie," he said, the word breaking somewhere in his throat. It had nowhere to go.

He sat on the bench. He waited — because he was built for waiting, especially for her.

He told himself a story about a girl with a paintbrush in her hair.

He told himself a story about a man who bought rings from antique shops because he believed in things that had lived other lives, the way some people believed in luck.

He waited in the grey until waiting was all that remained — his sleep as hollow as his waking life. And then he understood what the dream was telling him:

that sometimes, a door is closed on both sides.

He buried his face in his hands and sobbed until he was as dry as her canvas.

The park was silent. It held its breath and exhaled nothing, just like she had.

He pressed his fingers to his eyes, and light bloomed behind his lids like the last flare of a dying sun.

He didn't speak her name again; he couldn't bear to hear it fail.

He woke in the apartment where the fridge hummed and clicked, alive for the last time. The thermos stood on the sink like a soldier left at attention long after the battle had ended.

He took the ring from his pocket and set it on the table — he couldn't carry its weight anymore.

He pressed the button on the kettle, because that's what you do when there's nothing left to do.

He thought about the promise he'd made — noon, the bench — and the ones he never got to say — stay; let me take care of the parts that hurt.

The guilt pressed on his shoulders like Jupiter collapsing into a black hole.

He stared at the packet of DreamDoze — the irony not lost on him — and thought of her. His Dozy.

He took more than he ever had and lay down on the bed, on top of the covers, clutching the painting close to his chest, as if he'd fallen asleep reading.

As if he could make his leaving look like an accident he'd apologise for.

There are choices we tell ourselves we do not make.

He did not count.

He did not measure.

He understood only the idea of down.

He closed his eyes and aimed himself toward a park that might one day find its colour again.

"Posie," he whispered, because it seemed right to announce yourself when entering a room,

"I'm coming."

The apartment listened and said nothing.

Four o'clock.

The park found the bench warm in the day's sun, a thermos beside it, and a bunny tote resting in the grass.

The wind moved through, soft as breath, carrying a trace of flowers.

The lamppost stood upright — no longer leaning, no longer tired.

The colours had returned.

And on the bench sat Jake and Posie, hand in hand.

One with a ring on her finger,

and in his arms,

a painting.